The Bc

by Linda Koons • illustrated by L

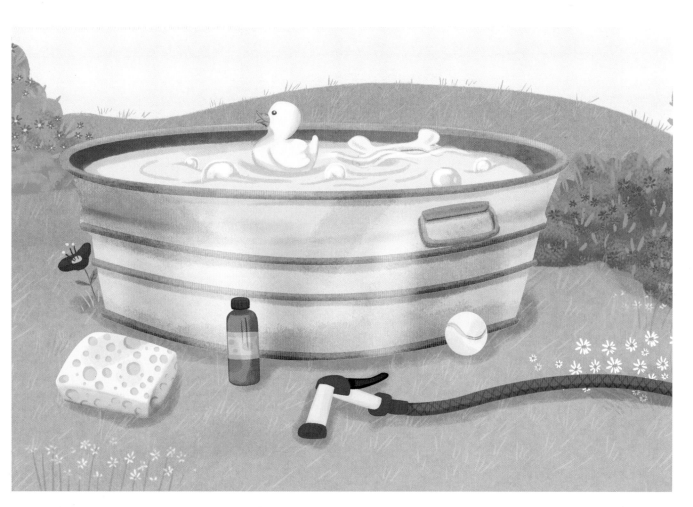

I put the water
in the tub.

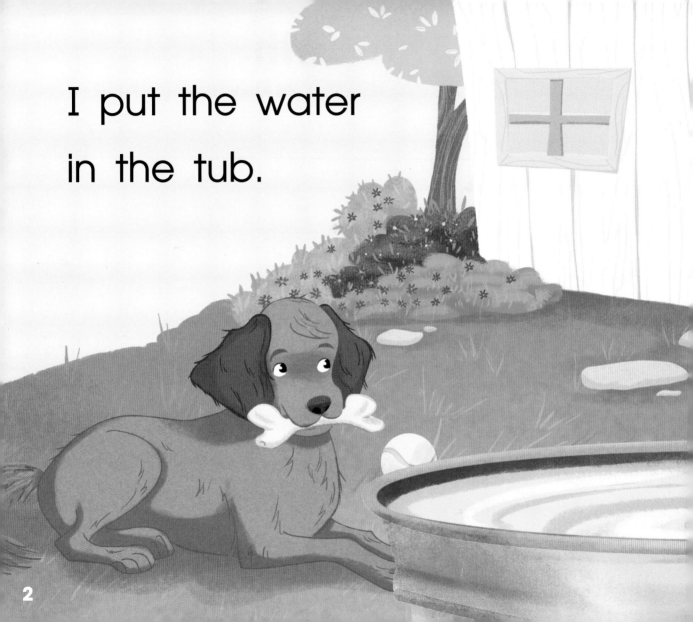

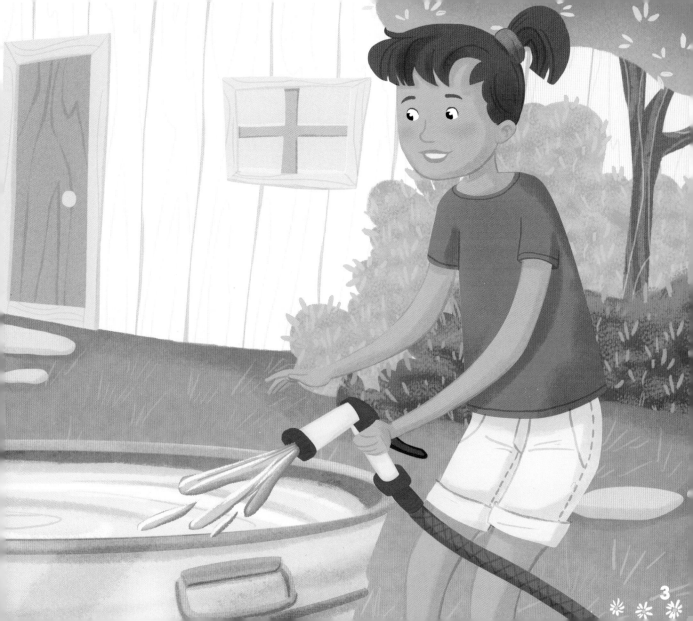

I put the soap
in the tub.

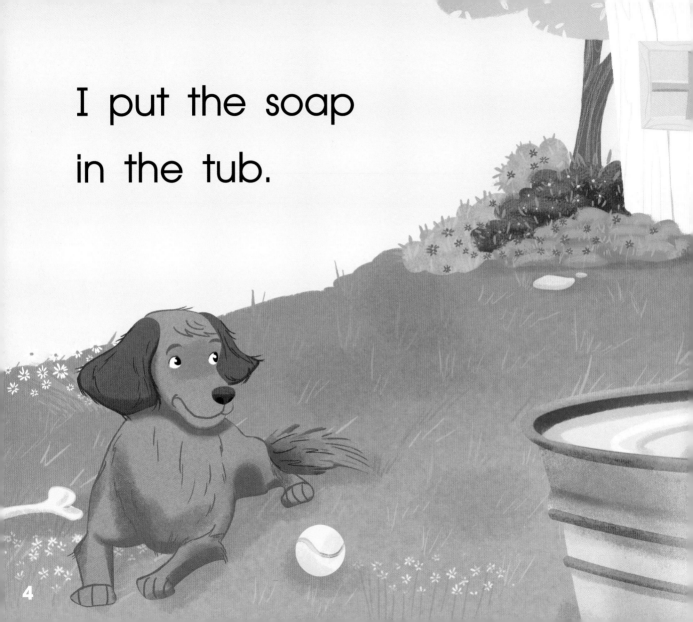

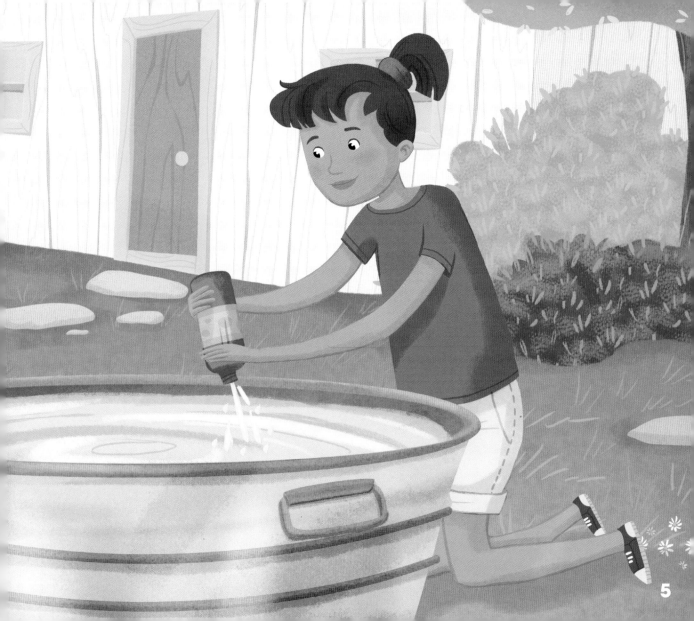

I put the sponge
in the tub.

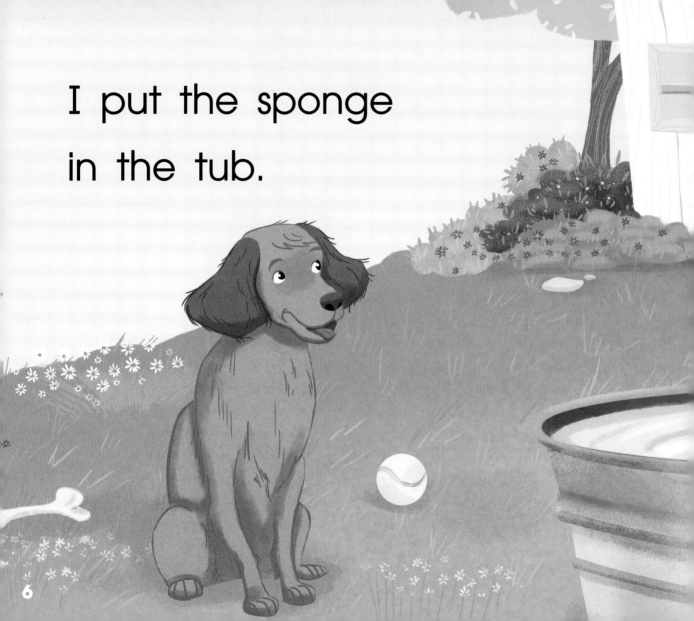

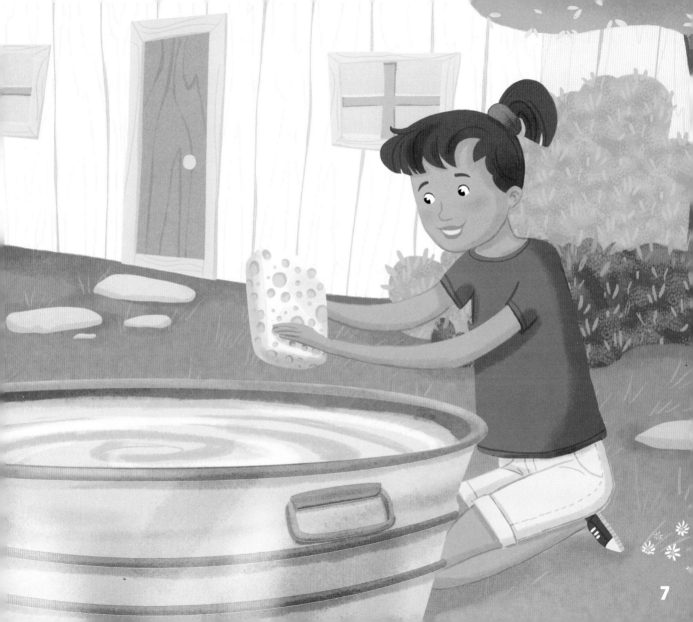

I put the duck
in the tub.

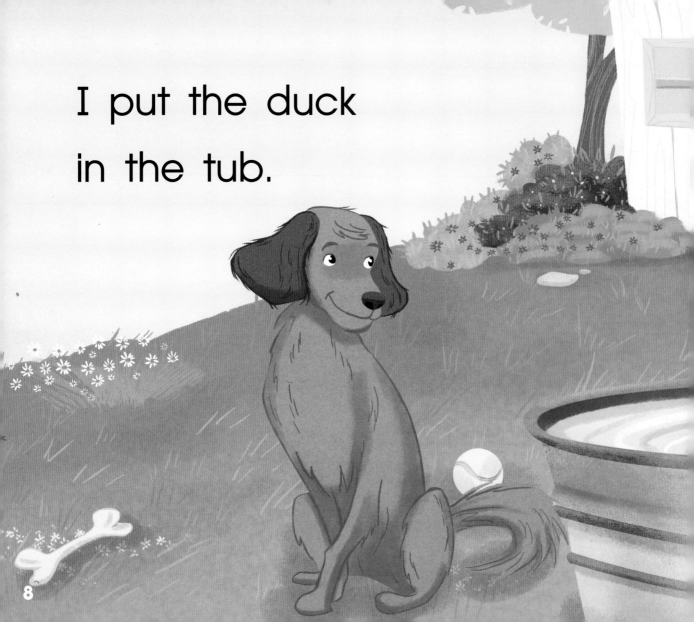

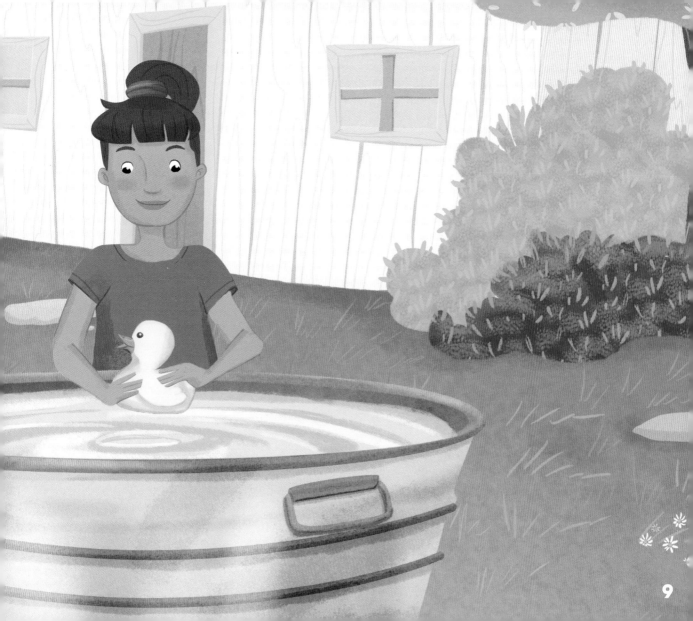

I put the bone
in the tub.

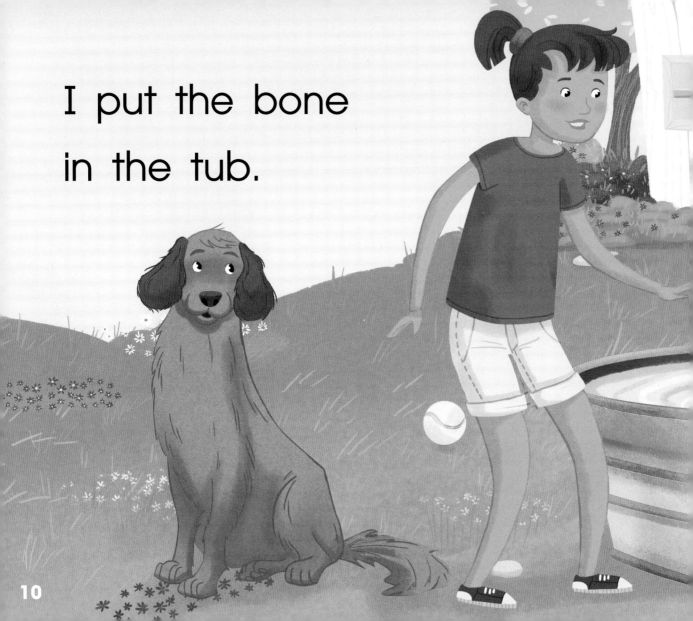

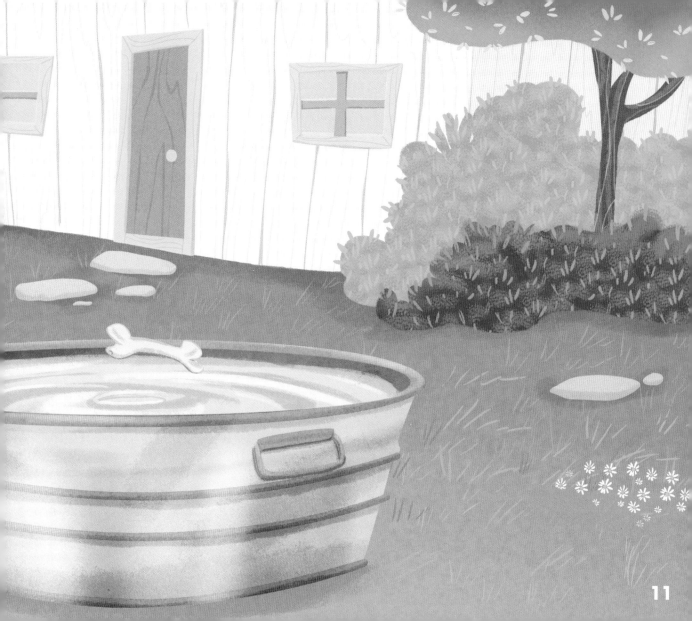

I put the ball
in the tub.

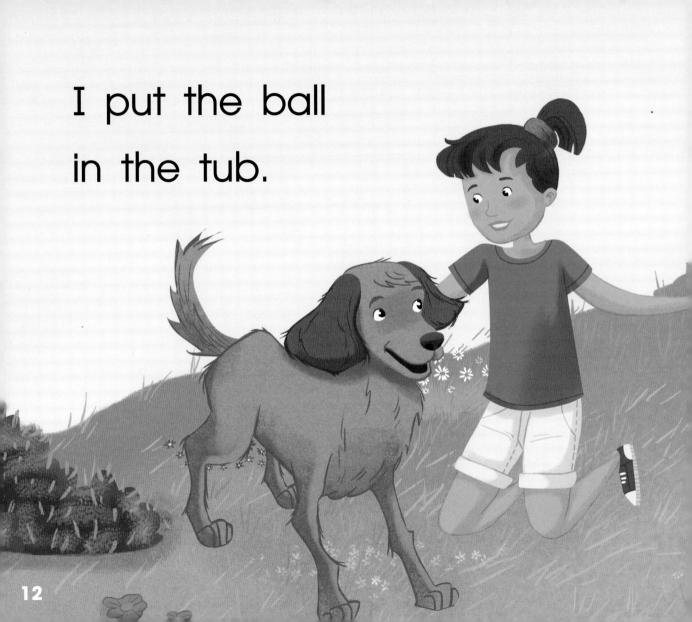

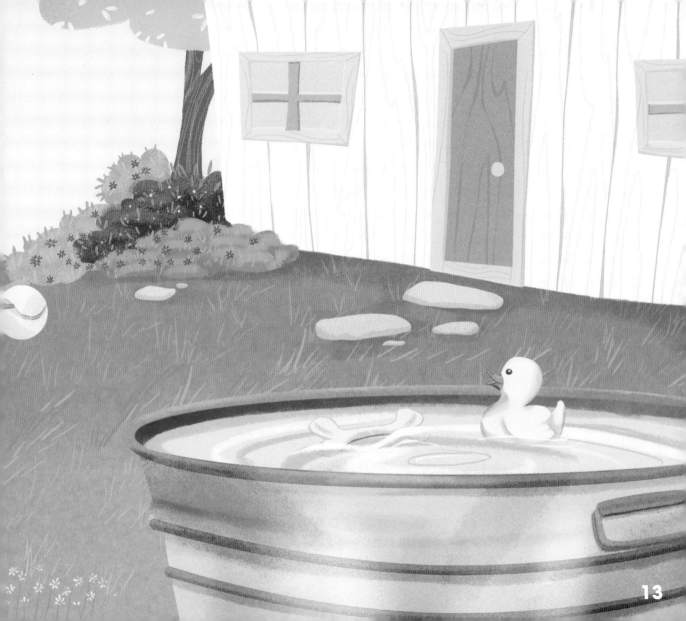

I put the dog
in the tub.

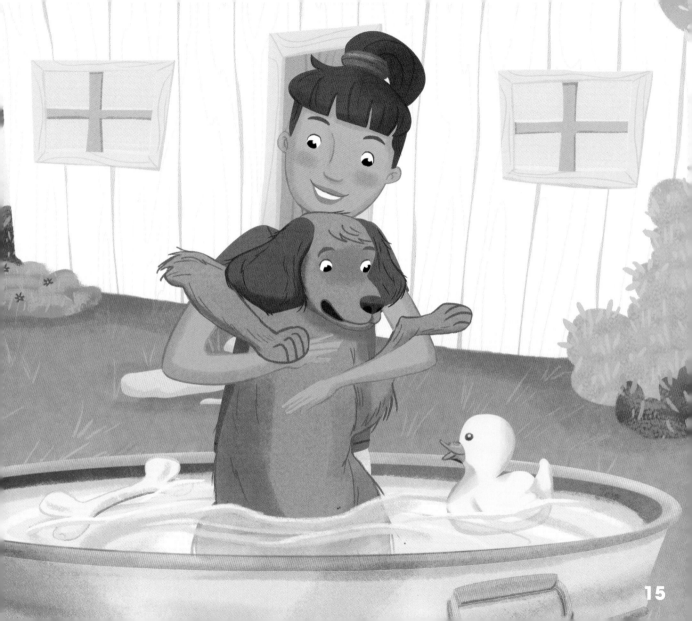

I get in the tub!

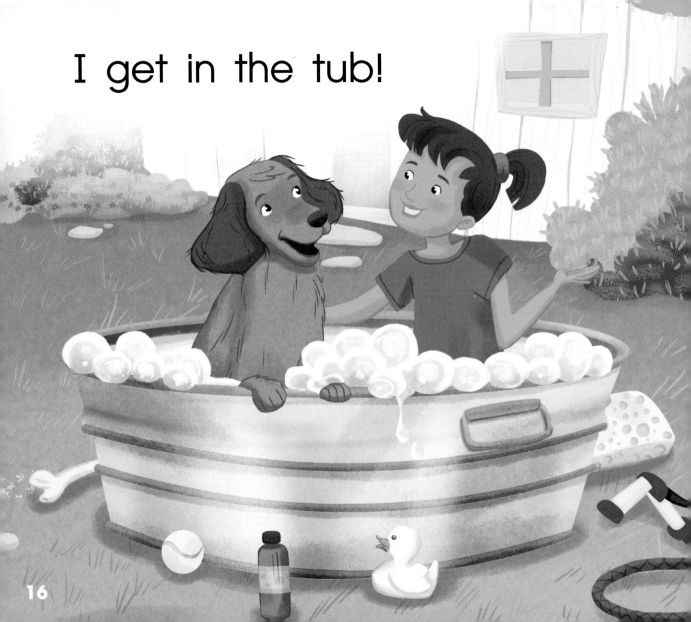